Put Beginning Readers on the F
ALL ABOARD READING

The All Aboard Reading series is especially for beginning readers. Written by noted authors and illustrated in full color, these are books that children really and truly *want* to read—books to excite their imagination, tickle their funny bone, expand their interests, and support their feelings. With four different reading levels, All Aboard Reading lets you choose which books are most appropriate for your children and their growing abilities.

Picture Readers—for Ages 3 to 6
Picture Readers have super-simple texts, with many nouns appearing as rebus pictures. At the end of each book are 24 flash cards—on one side is the rebus picture; on the other side is the written-out word.

Level 1—for Preschool through First-Grade Children
Level 1 books have very few lines per page, very large type, easy words, lots of repetition, and pictures with visual "cues" to help children figure out the words on the page.

Level 2—for First-Grade to Third-Grade Children
Level 2 books are printed in slightly smaller type than Level 1 books. The stories are more complex, but there is still lots of repetition in the text, and many pictures. The sentences are quite simple and are broken up into short lines to make reading easier.

Level 3—for Second-Grade through Third-Grade Children
Level 3 books have considerably longer texts, harder words, and more complicated sentences.

All Aboard for happy reading!

Text copyright © 1998 by Laura Driscoll. Illustrations copyright © 1998 by Ken Call. All rights reserved. Published by Grosset & Dunlap, Inc., a member of Penguin Putnam Books for Young Readers, New York. ALL ABOARD READING is a trademark of The Putnam & Grosset Group. GROSSET & DUNLAP is a trademark of Grosset & Dunlap, Inc. Published simultaneously in Canada. Printed in the U.S.A.

Library of Congress Cataloging-in-Publication Data is available.

ISBN 0-448-42040-6 (GB)   A B C D E F G H I J
ISBN 0-448-42039-2 (pbk.)   A B C D E F G H I J

ALL
ABOARD
READING™

Level 3
Grades 2-3

Slugger Season
McGwire and Sosa

By Laura Driscoll
Illustrated by Ken Call

With photographs

Grosset & Dunlap • New York

Number 62

September 8, 1998, 8:18 p.m.
Busch Stadium, St. Louis

It is the bottom of the fourth inning.
The Chicago Cubs are leading the St.
Louis Cardinals by a score of 2 to 0. But
right now, none of that matters. The
Cards' first baseman, Mark McGwire, has
just stepped up to the plate. Big Mac,
who is six-foot-five and 250 pounds of
power, takes a few easy practice swings.
Then he settles into his crouched batting
stance. The Cubs' pitcher, Steve Trachsel,
winds up and delivers the first pitch. In
an instant, the ball is over the plate and
McGwire lets loose with a mighty swing.

Crack! Is this the hit that everyone around the country has been waiting for? The ball rockets off McGwire's bat. It is a line drive headed deep into left field. But will it be high enough to clear the fence?

Yes! It's a home run. That's number 62! What's so special about that?

Mark McGwire has just made sports history. He has broken the major-league record for home runs in a single season— a record that stood for almost 40 years.

The home crowd goes wild and does not stop cheering for ten minutes. Fireworks explode over the stadium. McGwire himself is so excited as he rounds the bases that he almost misses first base. Even the Cubs' infielders high-five and hug McGwire as he trots past them. When McGwire comes across home plate, his entire team is there to meet him.

McGwire is not cocky, but for the last few days, he's been pretty sure this was going to happen. The right-handed slugger is so good at belting balls out of the park. Over his last 22 games, McGwire has hit 15 home runs.

McGwire's 62nd home run is one of the greatest moments in baseball history. But it is not the end of the 1998 story.

Sammy Sosa, the 29-year-old outfielder for the Chicago Cubs, also breaks the old record of 61 home runs in one season. It happens only five days after McGwire's historic homer, in an afternoon game against the Milwaukee Brewers.

Now the question is: Who will have hit the most home runs at the end of the '98 season?

The Sultan of Swat

It may seem hard to believe today, but baseball wasn't always a game of home runs and power hitters. At least, not until Babe Ruth came along.

George Herman Ruth was born in 1895. He began playing major-league baseball in 1914. He certainly did not look like a baseball superstar. He was big and round. But he was quick. And boy, could he hit home runs.

Babe Ruth
with fans in
the early days

In the early days of major-league baseball, most players hit fewer than five home runs in a season. Why so few?

Mostly it was because of the ball. Before 1920, the baseball was made differently

A major-league game in 1917

than it is today. It wasn't as lively. And it didn't fly as far. That's why those years are known as the Dead Ball Era. Most batters didn't even try to hit balls out of the park.

Babe, however, made that "dead ball" look pretty lively. In 1919, he hit a record 29 home runs for the Boston Red Sox. That was a lot for those days. But Babe was just getting warmed up.

In 1920, teams switched to the new, livelier baseball. And the Babe switched teams. He was sold to the New York Yankees. Right away, Babe Ruth showed everyone in New York just how far that new ball could fly.

In 1920, he hit 54 homers, almost doubling his old record.

In 1921, he hit 59, another record.

Fans called him the Sultan of Swing, the Wizard of Whack, the Colossus of Club, and the Bambino. The new home for the team, Yankee Stadium, was called The House That Ruth Built. People who had never liked baseball before started coming to games just to see the Babe hit one out of the park. Never before had a player hit 'em so hard and so far so often.

Babe's biggest home-run year was 1927. On the last weekend of the season, he hit his 60th homer. Fans cheered, but they weren't surprised. They were used to Babe's big bat by now. Would he go over sixty the next year?

Babe Ruth with a fan in Yankee Stadium

No. But over the next eight years, the Babe kept right on swinging. By the time he retired in 1935, he had knocked out a total of 714 home runs. And he had changed baseball forever.

The M & M Boys

In the summer of 1961, two more New York Yankees were racking up the home runs. People thought either one of them might break Babe Ruth's record.

They were Mickey Mantle and Roger Maris. The M & M boys, they were called. They were good hitters and good friends.

Roger Maris (left) and Mickey Mantle

Fans loved center fielder Mickey Mantle. He had played for the Yankees for ten years. If a player was going to break Babe's record, New York fans hoped it would be Mantle, not newcomer Maris. Maris had only been a Yankee for a year. He was shy and quiet. He was not a crowd pleaser like Mantle.

Then, at the end of September, Mantle was out of the race with a bad hip. He could not play for the rest of the season.

Now all eyes were on Maris. But many sports fans were rooting against him. When Maris stepped up to the plate, the fans booed.

Still, Maris kept on hitting home runs. Sure the pressure got to him. Before a game, he would pace back and forth in the locker room. "If I sat in front of my locker, my stomach turned to knots,"

Maris said. He kept to himself even more.
He stayed away from reporters. He was
under so much stress, his hair started to
fall out.

But in the very last game of the '61 season, Maris hit his 61st home run. It was a longer season than in Babe Ruth's time. Maris broke the record in 162 games. Babe had scored his 60 homers in only 154 games. Still, Maris set a new record fair and square. And one that stayed in the books for the next 37 years.

Roger Maris hitting his 61st home run

The Great '98 Season

The 1998 season started out like any other. Fans watched and waited to see which teams would jump out to a strong start. The 1997 World Series champions, the Florida Marlins, had been the newest team ever to win the World Series. The team had only been formed four years before. But after the '97 season, the Marlins had traded away their best players. The '98 championship was up for grabs.

Almost from opening day, the New York Yankees were making news. They won game after game, with one of the best all-around teams in their history.

But the '98 Yankees had no home-run sluggers like past Yankee legends Ruth, Mantle, and Maris.

Did any team have a big home-run hitter?

Yes. The St. Louis Cardinals. The team was having a rough season. But they had 34-year-old Mark McGwire. McGwire had homered 52 times in 1996 and 58 times in 1997. He was amazingly strong with huge, Popeye arms. He was also a consistent, dependable batter—the kind who waited for the right pitch. Each year, he was getting closer and closer to the record.

If only he could stay injury-free. McGwire had had various injuries in the past, which caused him to miss many games. In fact, from 1993 to

1995, he missed a total of 290 games because of injuries.

But 1998 seemed to be a lucky year. McGwire's health was good and by the end of July, he'd racked up 45 homers.

Then there was the Cubs' Sammy Sosa. Sosa was already famous in his

home country of the Dominican Republic. In 1998, he became a sports hero in the U.S. for belting line drives out of the park. By August, he had hit 42 home runs.

The Mariners' Ken Griffey, Jr. and the Padres' Greg Vaughn were also having strong seasons.

Of all these hitters, Greg Vaughn was the biggest surprise. Through 1997, Vaughn had trouble with his hitting. The Padres even tried to trade him.

But 1998 was different. By the end of July, Vaughn had hit 38 home runs. He ended the season with a total of 50.

Greg Vaughn

Ken Griffey, Jr.

Ken Griffey, Jr. kept saying that he was not a home-run hitter. But no one believed that anymore. In 1997, Junior was the American League MVP and he hit 56 home runs—only five short of Roger Maris's record.

In 1998, Griffey hit a whopping 14 home runs in the month of June alone. By early August, he had belted 41 homers. At the end of September, he had a season total of 56 again.

But it was Sammy Sosa who stayed hot on McGwire's trail. All through the month of August, McGwire and Sosa were neck and neck. It was the battle of the bats.

On August 19, Sosa hit home run number 48. The same day, McGwire hit his 48th and 49th homers—both in one game. Over the next few weeks, Sosa and McGwire traded homers. On August 31, the two players were tied for the lead at 55. But the next day, McGwire hit two more—56 and 57—in the same game, and then two more again—58 and 59—in the next game.

Reporters called it "the race within the chase"—the race to break Roger Maris's 1961 record. But it was a friendly race. McGwire and Sosa were rooting for each other. Sosa gave McGwire a big hug after McGwire hit his 62nd homer. Sosa jogged in from the outfield to greet his friend. "You did it!" he cried. And five days later, McGwire was just as happy when Sosa hit his 62nd homer.

All along both players kept saying it was more important that they help their teams win games. Not that they break the record for themselves. "Anything you can do to help the team get a victory is very, very special," McGwire said.

On Friday, September 25, going into the last weekend of the season, McGwire and Sosa were tied at 65 homers. That night, each of them homered to tie again at 66. Then McGwire really turned up the heat. He hit four home runs in his last two games of the season. McGwire had reached the unbelievable total of 70. Sosa finished with 66, and helped the Cubs win a spot in the playoffs.

People will remember both McGwire and Sosa when they think back to 1998. Because of them, fans all over the country witnessed an amazing chapter in sports history.

Here is a graph that shows the number of home runs each player hit over the course of the 1998 season.

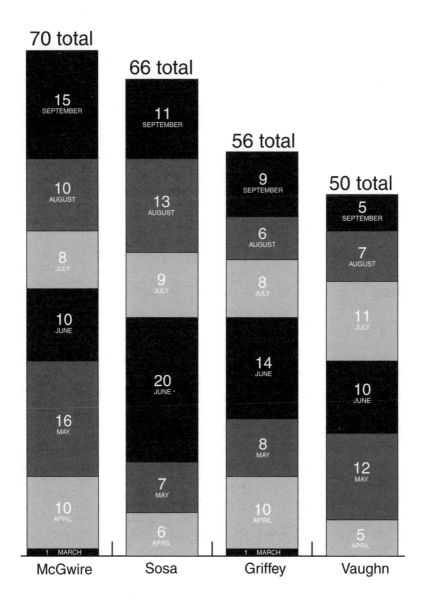

Little Mac

Mark McGwire was born on October 1, 1963. Even as a kid in Claremont, California, he was hitting homers. It is said that McGwire hit a home run the first time he came up to bat in a Little League game. He was only eight years old. Three years later, he set a Claremont Little League record with 13 home runs in one season. It was the first of many home-run records that McGwire would break.

On his college team at the University of Southern California, McGwire set a record in the Pac-10 conference with 32 home runs in a season.

In 1984, as a rookie for the Oakland A's, McGwire hit 49 home runs. This shattered the old rookie-season record of 38.

After more than ten years with the
Oakland A's, McGwire was traded to the
St. Louis Cardinals in 1997. The fans in
St. Louis welcomed the big slugger with
open arms. They loved McGwire. Not just
as a baseball superstar, but also as a
human being.

It is clear there are things that matter to
McGwire besides baseball. Back in 1987,
McGwire had a shot at hitting 50 home
runs—a big milestone. But with 49, he
took off the last game of the season to see
his son being born. Today, even though
McGwire is divorced, he spends as much
time as he can with his son, Matthew.

McGwire also gives generously to charities—especially ones that help children.

It's not just the fans who love Mark McGwire. He is admired and respected just as much by his fellow players—on and off the field. As his friend Sammy Sosa has said, "Mark is the man."

McGwire with his son Matthew, a Cardinal bat boy

Now Mark is not only the man; he's the new home-run king. Some people thought Roger Maris's record would stand forever. And before Maris, people thought Babe Ruth's record would never be broken.

How long will Mark McGwire's record stand? It may be decades before his record is broken...or it may happen as soon as next year!